Parent's Introduction

We Both Read Books are delightful stories which **both** a parent **and** a child can participate in reading aloud. Developed in conjunction with early reading specialists, the books invite parents to read the more sophisticated text on the left-hand pages, while children are encouraged to read the right-hand pages, which have been specially written for beginning readers. The parent's text is preceded by a "talking parent" icon: ; the children's text is preceded by a "talking child" icon: .

Educators know that nothing helps children learn to read more than by reading aloud with their parents. However, the concentration necessary for reading is often difficult for young children. That is why *We Both Read Books* offer short periods of reading by the child, alternating with periods of being read to by their parent. The result is a much more enjoyable and enriching experience for both!

Most of the words used in the child's text should be familiar to them. Others can easily be sounded out. An occasional difficult word will often be first introduced in the parent's text, distinguished with **bold lettering**. Pointing out these words, as you read them, will help familiarize them to your child. You may also find it helpful to read the entire book to your child the first time, then invite them to participate on the second reading.

We hope that both you and your children enjoy the *We Both Read Books* and that they will help start your children off on a lifetime of reading enjoyment!

We Both Read: The Tales of Peter Rabbit and Benjamin Bunny

THIS EDITION LICENSED BY FREDERICK WARNE & CO.

FREDERICK WARNE & CO. IS THE OWNER OF ALL RIGHTS
COPYRIGHTS AND TRADEMARKS IN THE BEATRIX POTTER
CHARACTER NAMES AND ILLUSTRATIONS.

Published by Treasure Bay, Inc.
40 Sir Francis Drake Blvd.
San Anselmo, CA 94960 USA

PRINTED IN SINGAPORE

Library of Congress Catalog Card Number: 97-62024

Hardcover ISBN 1-891327-01-1
Paperback ISBN 1-891327-30-5

05 06 07 08 09 / 10 9 8 7 6 5 4 3 2

We Both Read® Books
Patent No. 5,957,693

Visit us online at:
www.webothread.com

WE BOTH READ™

The Tales of
Peter Rabbit
&
Benjamin Bunny

Adapted by Sindy McKay

From the stories by Beatrix Potter

TREASURE BAY

Once upon a time there were four little Rabbits, and their names were —

> **Flopsy,**
>> **Mopsy,**
>>> **Cotton-tail,**
>>>> and **Peter**.

They lived with their **Mother** in a sand-bank, underneath the root of a very big fir-tree.

One day Mother told them to go out and play.

She told them to have fun.

She told them to be good.

"Now **Flopsy, Mopsy, Cotton-tail**, and **Peter**," said old Mrs. Rabbit, "you may go down the lane to gather **berries,** but don't go into Mr. McGregor's garden: your Father had an accident there; he was put in a pie by Mrs. McGregor."

Flopsy went to pick berries.

Mopsy went to pick berries.

Cotton-tail went to pick berries, too.

But not Peter.

Peter, who was very naughty, ran straight away to **Mr. McGregor's** garden!

He ate some carrots and French beans; and then, feeling rather sick, he went to look for parsley.

But round the end of a cucumber frame, whom should he meet but **Mr. McGregor**!

Mr. McGregor saw Peter. He was very, very mad!

Peter saw Mr. McGregor. He was very, very scared!

Mr. McGregor **jumped** up and ran after Peter, waving a rake and calling out, "Stop thief!" Peter rushed all over the garden, for he had forgotten the way back to the gate.

Peter ran and ran.

He ran very fast.

He ran so fast he lost his shoes!

A bird found one.

But it did not fit her.

Peter might have gotten away if he had not run into a net, and got caught by the large buttons on his jacket. Mr. McGregor came up with a sieve; to pop upon the top of Peter; but Peter wriggled out just in time, leaving his jacket behind him.

Peter had to hide.

He jumped into a can.

It was a good place to hide.

But it was full of water.

Mr. McGregor was sure that Peter was in the tool-shed, perhaps underneath a flower-pot. He began to turn them over carefully, looking under each.

Presently Peter sneezed—"Kertyshoo!" Mr. McGregor was after him in no time. Mr. McGregor tried to put his foot upon Peter, who jumped out of a **window.**

It was a very small window.

It was too small for Mr. McGregor.

So Mr. McGregor gave up.

Peter sat down to rest; he was out of breath and trembling with fright, and he had not the least idea which way to go. Also he was very damp with sitting in that can.

After a time he began to wander about, going lippity-lippity- not very fast, and looking all round.

Peter began to cry.

He wanted to go home.

But he did not know how to get there.

He tried to find his way straight across the garden, but he became more and more puzzled. Presently, he came to a pond where a white cat was staring at some gold-fish. Peter thought it best to go away without speaking to her; he had heard about cats from his cousin, little Benjamin Bunny.

Peter went back towards the tool-shed and climbed upon a wheelbarrow and peeped over.

Peter saw Mr. McGregor.

Behind Mr. McGregor was a gate.

Behind the gate was the way home!

Peter started running as fast as he could go. Mr. McGregor caught sight of him at the corner, but Peter did not care. He slipped underneath the gate, and was safe at last in the wood outside the garden.

Mr. McGregor hung up Peter's little jacket and shoes for a scare-crow to frighten the blackbirds.

Peter ran and ran.

He ran all the way home.

He lay down on the soft sand in his home.

And Peter went to sleep.

I am sorry to say that Peter was not very well during the evening.

His Mother put him to bed, and made some chamomile tea; and she gave a dose of it to Peter!

But Flopsy, Mopsy, and Cotton-tail had bread and milk and blackberries for supper.

The End

WE BOTH READ™

The Tale of
Benjamin Bunny

One morning a little rabbit sat on a **sandbank**.

Little **Benjamin** Bunny pricked his ears and listened to the trit-trot of a pony.

A carriage was coming along the road; it was driven by Mr. McGregor, and beside him sat Mrs. McGregor in her best bonnet.

Benjamin saw it go by.

Then he slid down the sandbank and
hopped away.

Benjamin went to call upon his relations. His aunt and cousins—Flopsy, Mopsy, Cotton-tail and Peter—lived in the wood at the back of Mr. McGregor's garden.

As he came round the back of their fir-tree, he nearly tumbled upon the top of his Cousin Peter.

Benjamin saw Peter.

Benjamin said hello to Peter.

Peter did not move.

Peter did not look happy.

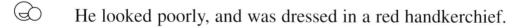 He looked poorly, and was dressed in a red handkerchief.

"Peter," said little Benjamin, in a whisper, "who has got your clothes?"

Peter replied, "The scarecrow in **Mr. McGregor's** garden," and described how he had been chased about the garden, and had dropped his shoes and coat.

Benjamin sat with Peter.

He told him Mr. McGregor was not home.

He told him Mr. McGregor was out for a ride.

Peter hoped that it would rain on Mr. McGregor.

Peter thought he might feel better if he went for a walk. So they went away hand in hand, and got upon the flat top of the wall at the bottom of the wood. From here they looked down into Mr. McGregor's **garden**. Peter's coat and shoes were plainly to be seen upon the scarecrow.

Benjamin jumped into the garden.

Peter *fell* into the garden.

But the garden was soft, so Peter was okay.

 Benjamin said that the first thing to be done was to get back Peter's clothes. They left odd little foot-marks all over the ground as they ran to take them off the scarecrow. There had been rain during the night; there was water in the **shoes,** and the **coat** was somewhat shrunk.

Peter put on his coat.

He put on his wet shoes.

Benjamin put on a great big hat!

Then Peter wanted to go.

But Benjamin did not.

Benjamin said he was in the habit of coming to the garden with his father to get lettuces for their Sunday dinner.

(The name of little Benjamin's papa was old Mr. Benjamin Bunny.)

Then he suggested that they should fill Peter's red handkerchief with onions, as a little present for his Aunt.

But Peter did not want to stay.

He did not want to be in the garden.

He did not think that this was fun.

Benjamin, on the contrary, was perfectly at home, and ate a lettuce leaf. Peter did not eat anything; he said he should like to go home.

Benjamin, with a load of vegetables, led the way boldly towards the other end of the garden.

Peter went with Benjamin.
But he did not like it.

Then Peter stopped.
He would not move.
He ***could*** not move.

Peter saw a CAT!

Benjamin took one look. In half a minute less than no time, he hid himself and Peter and the onions underneath a large basket …

The cat sniffed at the basket, then sat down upon the top of it.

She **stayed** there for *five hours*.

Peter wanted to go.

Benjamin wanted to go.

But the cat did *not* want to go.

So they all stayed.

At length there was a pitter-patter and some bits of mortar fell from the wall above.

The cat looked up and saw old Mr. Benjamin Bunny (young Benjamin's father) prancing along the top of the wall.

He had come for his son.
He had come for Peter.

He jumped off the top of the wall.
He jumped down on top of the cat!

Old Benjamin Bunny cuffed the cat off the basket, and kicked it into the green-house.

When he had driven the cat into the green-house, he locked the door.

Then he went to the basket, took out Benjamin and Peter, and marched them out of the garden.

Mrs. Rabbit was happy to see Peter.

She was happy to see his shoes and coat.

She told Peter **never** to go there again.

And Peter **never** did.

The End

**If you liked
The Tales of Peter Rabbit & Benjamin Bunny,
here are two other We Both Read™ Books
you are sure to enjoy!**

In this humorous and charming tale, a princess loses her golden ball and then makes promises to the frog who gets it back for her. But the princess does not want to keep her promises! To her surprise the frog appears at the castle door looking for the princess and all that she promised!

To see all the We Both Read books that are available,
just go online to **www.webothread.com**

    In this delightfully funny retelling or the classic
story, the emperor hires two tailors to make him an
elegant new set of clothes. The tailors say the clothes
are magical and that some people will think the
clothes are invisible. Can you guess what happens
when the emperor wears his new clothes?